The Travel Adventures of Bella & Anna

Do We Have to Move?

A children's book about the fun and fears of moving.

Written by Natalie Lee Martin

Illustrated by Tessa Diane Pray

All rights reserved.
Copyright © 2020 by Natalie Lee Martin

No part of this publication may be reproduced, stored in any retrieval system, or transmitted in any form or by any means, including photocopying, recording, or any other way without the written permission of the author.

We greatly appreciate you for buying an authorized copy of this book and for complying with the copyright laws by not reproducing, scanning, or distributing any part of this book in any form without permission. You are supporting the hard work of authors by doing so.

ISBN: (paperback): 978-1-7363011-2-8
ISBN: (hard cover): 978-1-7363011-0-4
ISBN (ebook): 978-1-7363011-1-1

To Isabella and Annalisse.

You are worthy of having all of you captured in a book.

Hello, my name is Bella.
My favorite color is pink and I love to dance. I also love to paint, draw, and play with my friends.

This is my sister Anna.
Her favorite color is purple and she loves to sing. Anna loves to play with me.
We play together a lot.

We live in our home with our mom, dad, and three older brothers.

My dad is in the United States Air Force. He's in the military and that means we always have to move.

Today, mom and dad told us that we are going to move again. We are always moving. Anna and I do not like to move.

The military told dad that we have to move overseas. That means we have to go to another country.

But Anna and I have decided that...

...we are not going to move.

Can you imagine all the bad things that will happen if we move?

First, we will miss our friends.
We have so much fun with our friends,
Avery and Amara.

We usually go to the park together and play on the swings, slide and seesaw.

Sometimes, we go to the pool together.

We even go on bike rides together.

When we can't visit each other, we often use our computers to talk to each other.

Maybe we can still talk to each other on the computer when we move. Then, we won't miss each other as much.

Secondly, we will have to go to a new school. Everyone knows how scary it can be when you are the new kid at school.

We will have a new teacher and we will have to make new friends. We will also have to learn a new language.

Oh, Daddy taught us a new language when Anna and I were much younger. Dad speaks Spanish and he taught us words like *hola*. That means hello. And *leche*. That means milk. It was so much fun. I like speaking *español*. That means Spanish.

Even though learning a new language and going to a new school may be fun, Anna and I have already decided...

...we are NOT going to move!

Lastly, we have to take two planes to get to our destination. We do not like planes.

Last year, our family had to take a plane to Puerto Rico for our summer vacation. We had lots of fun. We went hiking, horseback riding, and swimming. I loved swimming the most. The beaches were beautiful and the water was crystal clear. That means we could see right to the bottom of the ocean.

We could not have had such a great time if we did not take a plane. And besides, the pilot let us visit him in the cockpit. That's where the pilot sits to fly the plane. Maybe moving won't be so bad.

So, after we discussed all of our options, Anna and I have decided...

...we ARE going to move!

Daddy said we are going to Tokyo, Japan. Wow! Seems like that will be tons of fun. I am sure it will be. New language, new food, and a new culture. We can hardly wait!

We have to go pack our bags.
We are going to MOVE!

Anna and I are going on an adventure!

See you in Japan!

CPSIA information can be obtained
at www.ICGtesting.com
Printed in the USA
BVHW021825231220
596372BV00009B/20